# THE TREASURE OF GOLD MOUNTAIN

## STEFON MEARS

Thousand
Faces
Publishing

# Also by Stefon Mears

Published by Thousand Faces Publishing, Portland, Oregon

http://1kfaces.com



Front cover image © Alexfiodorov | Dreamstime.com (File ID: 14029628)



ISBN: 978-1-948490-56-6

# THE TREASURE OF GOLD MOUNTAIN

I knew there had to be dirt in there somewhere. I mean, I knew to *expect* some. If I'd found the right place. Plus, statistically speaking, the chances that the mountain in front of me was *entirely* made out of rock seemed pretty darned slim.

But I gotta say. From where I stood, I sure didn't see any dirt. Nothing green or even brown or yellow growing on the mountainside either.

I was standing on a low ledge of yellowish-brown rock, that had been warmed by the sun. Impressively warmed, considering it was still a couple of hours before noon. I could already *taste* that warmth in the dry, dusty air. Made me want to reach for my canteen, but not yet. I had to conserve water, for what I had in mind.

Probably going to be a very hot day, though. Not too surprising for Mexico in the summertime – no, I won't tell you where in Mexico I was, so let's just call it a *remote* part of that beautiful country and leave it at that, all right? – but still, I'd been back home *just* long enough this time to get used to Oregon weather again.

And in Oregon, even during high summer the sun wasn't strong enough to heat rocks as big as this ledge until late in the day.

Made me glad I had plenty of sunscreen. I'd more than earned my tan over years of haunting the more obscure regions of our globe for – well, we'll get to that part. Point is, I was lean and mean and tan from traveling to forgotten places and doing things that sane men don't do.

But that's only because sane men don't know how to have fun. Or maybe just have no sense of adventure. You can make the call for yourself, if you're one of them.

Me, well, I'm the one talking, so I'll get back to it.

And I mention the tan because even a tan as deep as mine could still burn, if I weren't careful.

So I was standing on yellowish-brown rock and staring up at what looked to be over a mile of more of the same, only sloping sharply toward the vertical instead of maintaining a roughly horizontal position.

I'd spent the past ten minutes just gazing at it from below. Long enough that I felt at least *pretty* sure I had the right place. Sure enough to keep going.

Wasn't easy finding this mountain, but all my cross-referencing – not to mention the maps I consulted from different eras – had led me to this general area. And while this particular mountain wasn't the *only* contender for my target, it came closest in terms of the right *look*.

Just enough yellow in the brown of the rock that at sunrise, after a fresh rain, it could be mistaken for being made entirely of gold.

You know, from a pretty fair distance. When seen by a conquistador who *desperately* wanted to find something awesome to report back to his king and queen.

If I was right, then I had found Mexico's Montaña de Oro, or "Gold Mountain."

No, I don't expect you've heard of it. Even if you're a Mexican history buff.

While I'm pretty sure more than one mountain down in South America had been called Gold Mountain at some point, here in Mexico, there was exactly one. And it was called that by exactly one conquistador.

See, Gold Mountain – if this *was* Gold Mountain – was one of those finds obscure enough that most internet searches won't turn up even a single reference to it.

Of course, that's true of almost everything I go after.

The way I look at it, the only stuff worth finding these days requires real *work*. The kind of effort that takes me into dusty archives with old tomes or microfiche or worse – and requires me to fill in information gaps myself, solve riddles, and make difficult connections.

To put in less effort, well, that would be asking to "find" something well-known enough it might as well have a guidebook and gift shop by the time I got there.

Fate worse than death, if you ask me.

No. There are plenty of mysteries left in this wide, beautiful world. If you know where to look for them. And you have to be willing to do the legwork yourself.

And this mountain, if it was indeed Gold Mountain, had a heck of mystery waiting for me in its depths. Buried by an obscure conquistador named Miguel Vicente de la Cruz y Sangre.

Story goes that de la Cruz y Sangre found something *wonderful* in the heart of that mountain. But conflict with the ... well, let's just say the locals, because telling you if they were Aztecs or Maya or something else would clue you in on my location. Anyway, conflict with the locals came to a head and he had to leave the mountain and take charge of his people without claiming the treasure.

I'm not telling the general public where this was. I'll leave that for others. When they're ready.

Anyway, according to de la Cruz y Sangre's own notes, he buried his find. And even in his own notes, he wrote three conflicting reports about where exactly he buried it and never got more than vague about exactly what it was. Just in case someone *stole* those notes.

Which turned out to be what happened.

De la Cruz y Sangre died, fighting the locals. One of his people – Martín Zaragoza – survived to escape the carnage.

Well, arguably, you could reasonably conclude that Zaragoza deserted *during* the battle. Because apparently he came away with not only de la Cruz y Sangre's notes, but enough food and supplies to keep him going for quite some time.

Zaragoza didn't find the treasure, though. And on returning to Spain, he turned the notes over to his father confessor, while seeking absolution for his sins in the New World.

The father confessor added a couple of his own notes, and...

You get the idea.

Point is, if this was indeed de la Cruz y Sangre's Gold Mountain, then there was a chance that I'd be able to find something amazing hidden in its depths. And I was pretty sure that my six months of research had led me to the right place.

Just the thought of it got that good flutter going in my stomach, where I was standing on that rocky ledge, staring up at my goal.

Something amazing. Buried somewhere inside this giant slab of rock.

Which meant there had to be dirt in there somewhere.

Right?

---

THE ENTRANCE TO THE MOUNTAIN WASN'T DOWN AT GROUND LEVEL. Because *of course* it wasn't. If there'd been a nice, easy cave entrance down here at ground level, then *lots* of people would've gone inside it over the years. Even though the nearest river was…

Well, let's just say the nearest river wasn't *that* close.

No, even de la Cruz y Sangre had taken it as a sign from God that he hadn't had an easy time finding a way into the mountain. As though God had put this challenge in front of him to test him. The promise of a mountain made of gold to draw him near, then a true treasure waiting for him inside, once he found a way in.

If God was testing him though, he must've failed. Because he didn't survive to claim that treasure.

He did find a way into the mountain, though, on its north face. Which, admittedly, took me the better part of a day to get to from that spot on the rocky ledge. But just as I was ready to stop and make camp for the night, the afternoon sun showed me what I needed to see. What I'd hoped to spot.

A cross, chiseled into the rock at the foot of the mountain. Four feet high by maybe two-and-a-half feet wide. Exactly the marker de la Cruz y Sangre wrote that he'd left himself, so he could always find the entrance.

That meant that the entrance was about two hundred fifty feet up the mountainside. Give or take.

Too late in the day for me to check that out *now*, of course, but it meant I could get an early start the next day.

So I pitched my tent in the shadow of an overhanging boulder that was reasonably close to the cross – maybe two hundred feet or so – and prepared for one last night's sleep, before my hunt began in earnest.

Now, though the mountain itself seemed free of actual *dirt*, here at the foot there was plenty of dust around. Or loose, thin, dry dirt if you prefer. Whatever you call it, it was a good thing, and just what I needed.

My tent was already a boring beige. But this was a place where boring beige might stand out, if someone was looking for a tent. Say, from the sky.

So I patted my tent down with lots of dust, to camouflage it. Just in case one of my ... well, let's call them competitors. Enemies seems too *judgmental*, you know? So just in case one of my competitors had found out that I'm in the region and taken to the air to track me down.

Screw 'em. I don't do all that homework for someone else's benefit.

Well ... that's not *quite* true. In some ways I do. I mean, if I found the treasure somewhere inside Gold Mountain, wasn't like I was going to *keep* it. No, I'd contact the Mexican authorities, give them the treasure and my notes, and let whatever I found take its proper place in a museum.

A *Mexican* museum.

Of course, this attitude was one of the reasons I developed so many *competitors*. Not a lot of us who do this kind of treasure hunting, and most of those who do are after money. They'll sell to private collectors, or to the big-name museums. Basically to whoever can write the biggest, fattest check.

And those checks get big and fat enough that my competitors can bribe a *lot* of people. Which is the reason I have to work alone these days. I used to do things with a team, which was a good deal safer, let me tell you. But it seemed as though every find I tracked down either had a competitor waiting for me on arrival, or at least one hot on my heels.

My daddy used to tell me, "Clark, one time is bad luck. Two times is coincidence. Three times, that's enemy action."

So after the third time it happened, I started working exclusively alone. And gee, my competitors suddenly had a *much* harder time chasing down my leads.

Just as well, in some ways.

I do this because I love the experience of being the first person to find some wonderful thing. (Or even just the first person in hundreds of years, you know? Why pick nits?) Just me, and the discovery. Having other people around, well, all too often it diminished the experience. They always wanted to go straight to the business side of things, instead of savoring the magnificence of the moment.

And once I've had that experience, I think the right thing to do is hand the find over to the people who share in its history.

Not *sell* it to them. Not put it up for auction. Not even run to the press for credit. Just waltz into an appropriate office and hand it to them. *Fait accompli.*

I don't care about credit. And I don't really care about money.

I care about solving puzzles no one else has solved. About finding things no one else has found.

But I have to admit. I do take pleasure in seeing the dawning unbridled joy on an academic's face when they realize I've just *handed over* something they didn't even know was missing. Some new thing they can study, hell, even build a career writing about.

Those things, though, are secondary. What I was doing, that was primary.

And I no longer invited anyone else to the party.

So I did my best to hide my one-man tent, then retreated inside it for my simple dinner of beef stew reheated over Sterno, and a good night's rest.

And if you're wondering, yes, it *was* a good night's rest. I've slept on so many hard, rocky surfaces over the years that it's soft mattresses that give me trouble.

The next morning, I broke down my tent, then unfolded my field shovel and buried it. Not deep. Just enough to keep anyone from casually spotting it. If anyone actually *searched* the area, they'd find my tent quickly enough. But if they'd tracked me this far, that four-foot cross would be the bigger clue where I'd gone than the tent could ever be.

Plus, it was good to start the day with a little exercise. Loosen up the muscles, before the climb.

Only dawn, and already the night's vague chill was gone. Today looked to be even hotter than yesterday, and yesterday had cost me more water than I liked. Not more than I'd *planned* on, but more than I liked.

The skies were clear. Good and bad, that. On the one hand, it was good climbing weather, which was a plus. On the other, it was also good flying weather. Which meant I had to be careful, and as quick as possible, on my way into the mountain.

Quick, I could only do so much about. Couldn't see the entrance from down here. No idea if anyone could see the entrance from above. Assuming they knew to look for it, which I didn't consider *too* likely. I'd done a good job, hiding my research trail.

That's one of the irritating parts about having *competitors*. We all watch each other, or have others do it, so researching any given target means pretending to research a half-dozen others as a smokescreen.

Fortunately, I figured out a couple of years ago how to do *partial* research on other interesting topics, while disguising both them and the main topic of my homework.

Meant I usually had two or three projects underway, to one extent or another. Also made it harder for anyone to track what I was after at any given moment.

No, there was always a chance that someone had managed to track my *movements* when I came down here. That part, I could do only so much to prevent. But I was confident that anyone who followed me wouldn't know what I was after.

So any overhead plane would be looking for *me*.

And *that* I could do something about.

I was wearing a khaki shirt and cargo shorts, with a matching pack. And I covered myself and my pack with more of that yellowish-brown dust. Especially my hair. My tanned skin might not be too eye-catching, seen small and through binoculars, but my short, auburn hair and Van Dyke sure would be.

Once I was as covered as I reasonably could be, without getting to the point that I'd risk falling over a sneeze or cough, I was ready to make my ascent.

One thing I didn't know was how de la Cruz y Sangre had made his own first ascent. I knew that he'd had a scaffold built later – or at least partially built, because I don't know that it was finished – with the intention of using it to extract the mountain's riches. Which, if I could trust this part of his notes, *did* include some gold.

Whatever method he'd used for his own first ascent, though, was so well-known to him that he must've considered it too obvious to be worth writing down.

Me, I did it the way most modern climbers would attempt it – free soloing. No pitons, no rope, nothing but hands and feet.

Fortunately, the rock face was irregular enough to give me plenty of hand- and footholds, braces, and the like.

And by the time the sun was fully up and peeking at me between other mountains of the range, I'd covered my two-hundred-fifty-feet-plus of mountainside and found what had to be the entrance.

It was an opening behind a up-jut, with a slight overhang of rock above it. I even found what might have been fibers of rope used by de la Cruz y Sangre and his people, to aid their ascents.

I took pictures of the fibers where they were, then collected them with tweezers and put them in a plastic bag, along with a card on which I wrote what they were, along with precise GPS coordinates and a description of where I found them.

I hadn't done that kind of thing the first couple of times I'd hunted down lost treasure. Damn near got myself murdered by academics, screaming about technique and lost information.

Nowadays, well, my technique probably still wasn't up to the requirements of formal archeology and anthropology, but it was good enough that years had passed since someone had physically attacked me for it.

Yes, that happened once. In Vienna. Long story.

Just as I snapped that last pic, I heard the distinctive sound of Cessna Aerobat. Just the kind of small plane favored by people of my calling. Very maneuverable. And modified correctly, it needed only a very short runway for takeoffs and landings.

I ducked inside the opening, put my back to the rock wall and crouched. Hands over my hair and beard.

I watched the sky carefully.

Sure enough. Cessna Aerobat. Dusky orange-red color. Didn't recognize it, but that didn't mean anything. The way it flew was all I needed to know.

It flew low, between the peaks. Trying to make a grid pattern of them. Like it was looking for someone.

Like it was looking for *me*. Because it'd be a hell of a coincidence of someone else just happened to be in the area right now.

I think I went deeper before anyone on the Cessna could have spotted me. But if they had a spotter with good enough binoculars, there was no way to be sure.

Time might be of the essence. I turned and went deeper into the mountain.

---

LED LIGHTS ARE ONE OF MY FAVORITE MODERN INNOVATIONS. THEY don't need much power to provide an impressive number of lumens. They don't burn out easily. And they can be tuned to imitate specific kinds of light.

The one I wore strapped to my forehead was tuned for daylight. Bright and crisp and clear, and soothing on a deep, emotional level.

And let me tell you. A little subliminal soothing was a good thing, when delving alone into a mountain.

See, going deep inside millions of tons of rock all by oneself brings an awareness with it.

Isolation, yes, but also, a deep sense of awe. The sheer scope of it. The size. And the weight.

And in this case, that all those millions and millions of tons of rock were held together by a natural formation. That this tunnel I walked down – this apparently natural arch in the rock maybe two strides across and just tall enough that I couldn't *quite* stretch up and touch the top – was the only thing keeping me getting flattened so thoroughly I'd go from three-dimensional to two.

At least, I *thought* this was a natural tunnel. I'd checked the sides and couldn't find any obvious gouges or other tool marks. But geology had never been my area of expertise.

I admit, though, that I preferred to think it was a natural tunnel. Because if it *were*, then it had likely held this shape from that time eons ago when this mountain first formed.

If that were true, then it seemed to me that if it'd held together that long, it would hold together at least long enough for me to get in and out. I mean, barring some kind of major earthquake or something.

Which was a possibility...

Not the direction I needed to be thinking right now.

No, if it were natural, I'd probably be fine. If it had been carved or widened or shaped by human hands, though, those hands could have introduced a flaw that by now could get exacerbated by even the tread of a single interloper – a single big, if well-toned interloper, carrying a fairly significant weight of pack on his back – and trigger just the kind of reaction that would end my career real quick.

So I kept telling myself that I was following a natural tunnel. Maybe a channel that had been cut by water sometime before Egypt established its first dynasty, and would remain just the way it was until long after I was dead.

Heck, for a while, it was easy enough to believe. For the first several hundred feet of that tunnel, following what I thought was a slow but steady incline at a slow, but steady pace – an incline I took as more evidence that water had dug this tunnel, not human hands – I didn't see *any* signs that humans had ever been here before me.

Don't get me wrong. I wasn't expecting skeletons or fast food wrappers. But I figured that if de la Cruz y Sangre had ever gotten as far as building that scaffolding, then surely I'd find...

Then again, I didn't find any evidence of that scaffolding, did I? Just that cross, cut into the rock. So maybe he never got beyond the planning stage? Maybe the initial steps of building? I mean, two hundred fifty feet of scaffolding would have to leave *some* evidence, even hundreds of years later.

If he'd built it.

Which suggested that he'd died before he'd built it. Unless...

Unless the locals had torn the scaffolding down and demolished it.

Oh, *that* was an unpleasant thought. Because if the locals went to that much effort to destroy something the Spaniards had built, it was either because they *couldn't* use it or they *wouldn't* use it.

Couldn't, obviously, wasn't likely. I mean, the locals used gold, and supposedly there was some in here to find.

Which meant it was *more* likely that the locals *wouldn't* use that scaffolding.

Which suggested that this mountain, or something inside it, had held special significance to the locals. Which, most of the time, meant *religious* significance.

Lovely.

Mind you, I didn't *mind* entering someplace that was said to be religiously significant. Hell, if I cut out *those* sites from my options, I'd lose at least half my potential targets.

Still. I preferred to at least know in advance. So I could study the local practices of the era. Learn what the taboos were. I preferred to be as respectful as possible, when I did my thing.

Well, too late for that now. If I'd violated some taboo by coming here at high summer, or during the daytime, or without following the proper rituals first, then I had. Done is done.

All the same, I offered a quick and sincere apology to the ancients who might once have trod these tunnels as part of some important ceremony, and had to hope they'd understand that my intentions, at least, were as honorable to their memory and their descendants as I could make them.

In case you're wondering, I wasn't especially worried about the possibility of curses. Yes, I knew the stories that had spread about the great curses of Egypt, and how many members of which archeological teams had suffered from those curses and so forth.

But I had no reason to believe that I was at a burial site, or anything equivalent, that might've made the locals take those sorts of measures.

As to whether or not *curses* are real, well, let me just say that we don't understand everything about this world just yet. So I don't *worry* about such things, but I don't entirely discount them either.

Because the "magic" behind a curse could just as easily be some chicanery or chemistry or similar that we don't have reason to expect.

One man's "curse" could easily be another man's carefully laid and subtle trap. And might just involve chemicals that could last a long, long time.

Enough about that though.

Point is, I was following that tunnel into the mountain. Smelling nothing but dusty rock. Though it was, at least, *cooler* dusty rock than I'd have smelled outside under that summer sun. And the remains of my breakfast protein and granola bar – which was supposed to taste like cherries, but didn't quite manage the feat – might've lingered on my teeth and tongue, but not so much in my belly. Which meant I'd been up and working for … maybe six hours at that point, much of it continuing down that tunnel. Though some of it checking the sides and rocky ground for signs that humans had been here before me. Some little bit of stone or metal, or maybe wood or leather, that I could bring back to those academics, along with the treasure I hoped to find.

So far, though, I'd found no evidence at all refuting the idea that I was the first human being to get this far into this mountain...

...until I reached that bridge.

---

THE TUNNEL HAD LED ME TO A CREVASSE, MAYBE ... SIXTY FEET ACROSS. No meaningful ledge on this side or the other. Instead of a nice, neat arch above me, the rock walls looked to come together a few hundred feet up from where I stood. Hard to be sure. My light only gave me reliable vision out to ... hundred fifty feet. If that.

The crevasse looked to go down a long, long way, too. Didn't know exactly how far, but it definitely a fatal distance. If I fell.

And spanning the gap of this crevasse, a bridge. Most of one, at least.

Once upon a time, there had been a bridge of stone and wood and rope spanning this crevasse. Stone, where it anchored on each side. Wood for planks and rails and part of the frame to hold them. Rope, holding those planks together, and here and there tying them to the handrails, so the whole bridge couldn't be brought down at once.

The handrails, of course, where also bound to the top of the frame, a single arching piece of wood that socketed into stone on each side.

Huh. The handrails also socketed into stone. Not on the rockface, like the top part of the frame, but into the carved stone that anchored both ends. They weren't arched, though. Straight.

This had to have been built by locals. Because I doubted the Spaniards would've used both stone and wood for the structure. One or the other, more likely.

In this case, wood, not stone. After all, those Spaniards had been under the command of de la Cruz y Sangre, and from the tenor of his notes, that man had been in something of a hurry.

Not to mention that I doubted he'd brought any stonemasons with him. And the remains of the stonework – which, as far as I could tell, was entirely intact – had been lovingly crafted out of the rockface of what had once been a slightly longer ledge on each side.

The planks were gone. Someone had done a thorough job of cutting them free, even slashing the mid-bridge ropes that had bound the planks to the handrails.

Sisal, for the rope, by the way. Not hemp. Which reinforced my idea that the locals had built this bridge.

Might well have been the locals who took it down, too. Because the planks were long gone, and the remains of the rope on this end –

a thick loop around the stone foundation – had been cut by some-thing very, very sharp.

Cut at both ends, as well as along the middle, because otherwise I would've seen the remains of those planks and rope hanging from the other side. But that side looked to have been cut free, same as this one.

The wooden handrails were still in place, though, and still tied to that top arching frame support. I couldn't help but wonder if that was because they didn't have time to bring them down too. Or if there was some other reason they'd been left in place...

Either way, all three – the two rails and the top support – looked to have been made from tree trunks about as big around as my fore-arm. Maybe a *little* bigger for the top support, but not much.

Now, my muscles are pretty good, but that's still not very thick. And in my opinion, it was asking a lot for that wood to support a bridge.

Of course, that would depend a bit on what they'd wanted this bridge for. Also, what *kind* of wood it was. In this case, maybe oak or pine. I couldn't be sure, unless I got to look at the grain. Either way, the wood was *old*. In a very dry climate. Which might mean brittle.

Which might mean those handrails would snap under the weight of even one Clark Taggart.

Well, this was why I brought plenty of rope of my own. And a grappling hook.

The rope I used for this was a good, dynamic type. That kind that would stretch to absorb some of my weight if I fell.

I wasn't happy about using the grappling hook, though. I mean, I needed it. No question. It was just that, for security, I'd have to hook the stone on the other side. And that stone was some archeologist's or anthropologist's wet dream. They wouldn't look kindly on my gouging or scuffing the surface – possibly even damaging some bit of decorative artwork – just to preserve something as historically insignificant as my own life.

In other words, I wouldn't tell them. But I'd still feel bad about it.

Speaking of those academics, though, before I started unwinding rope and so forth, I stopped and took a whole lot of pictures. And some video. And made notes about my estimate of how far I'd come into the mountain when I'd found this.

Couldn't give them exact GPS coordinates, of course. Hard to get a signal, surrounded by millions of tons of rock.

But after I'd done my due diligence to preserve what I knew for future generations, I prepped my rope and grappling hook, and let that hook fly.

I hit a snag, and not the good kind.

Oh, don't get me wrong. My grappling hook caught and caught firmly.

To a coil of rope *around* one of the stones that had once supported the bridge slats.

And the blades had cut in deep enough that I couldn't get it free.

Not what I would call an ideal result. Because I had no idea if the rope would hold. And if it didn't, no way to tell if the spot I'd hooked would grasp the stone or skate right off.

But that was the drawback to doing these things on my own. Yes, I didn't have to share the joy of the discovery with anyone, but it also meant I didn't have anyone to help mitigate the risks, either.

Ah, well. Nothing for it but to keep moving.

At least the academics couldn't get mad at me for damaging their precious stonework.

I secured myself to the rope, stepped out onto the edge of the stonework, and began to work my way slowly across the remains of the bridge. Which meant I had my feet on what used to be a handrail and my hands on the arching top of the structure.

One slow step at a time, moving sideways to my right, I made my way across.

Mathematically speaking, I should've known I'd be in the exact middle when I had a problem. I mean, that was the spot where the rail would take the most stress, from my weight. Especially since the rail didn't have an arch, to help distribute my mass.

And that was where I was when I heard the first definite *creak*.

It's funny. All the exertion of the day, all the effort I was putting in right then, but I hadn't *noticed* myself sweating until I heard that creak.

I wanted to go faster. I really did. But that would've increased my risk. Sent more and faster vibrations through the wood than my slow, steady pace did.

No, my best chance was to ignore my sweat, and the dryness of my mouth, and the way my heartrate had sped like I was trying to catch a Formula One racer on foot, and just keep my slow, steady pace.

Life should reward a person who keeps his cool – more or less – in moments like that. Shouldn't it?

Alas, life disagreed with me that time.

I'd gotten maybe two steps farther when the handrail snapped with the kind of brittle crack that suggested that the whole bridge was actually just so much kindling.

I had barely enough warning to start jumping upward before the remains of the handrail fell away beneath me.

Oh, it was still tied to the top of the frame in at least a couple of places. Though the nearest ties had broken when the wood gave way. And the far ends of the handrail popped out of their stone supports.

So now the remains of that rail hung there. Loose. Useless. Mocking me.

I also hung there, over the crevasse. Feeling almost as useless myself, in the moment. My right arm hooked around the top support of the bridge frame. Not a good long term solution, because my shoulder and elbow would start complaining soon.

I needed a way out of this, and my options weren't great.

I swung my legs up, trying to hook my ankles over. Took me a couple of tries, but I managed it.

All right. Now I was getting somewhere. I could crawl across this way. Wouldn't be fast, but it should work as long as the ... tree, pole, whatever ... held out.

Only one problem.

See, that pole / tree / whatever I was crawling along, it was arched. And yes, it was anchored in stone at both ends, but not so deeply as I would've liked right then.

Apparently, the bridge designers had relied on the balanced counterweight of the two rails and their rope to hold the frame in place. And despite my feelings about it in the moment, it was probably the right call. Otherwise, they'd've had to cut the perfect slot even deeper into the rock, as well as cut down an even longer tree and so forth.

In the moment, though, their decision was my problem.

Hadn't been, when I'd first started across. The tension created by the ropes and handrails – with extra support from the handrails' sockets – had been enough to cope with the addition of my body weight, when my feet had been on one rail and my hands had been on the frame itself.

But I'd jumped onto the frame, just as one of those rails gave way. That changed the whole equation.

The frame itself began to slowly spin toward the intact handrail.

Nothing good could come of this.

I tried to correct. Tried to catch that other handrail with my feet, while still holding the frame top with my hooked arm.

Without the tension of the fallen handrail to help, this handrail wasn't ready for the sudden extra weight, so close to its middle. It, too, gave under my weight and broke free from its stone supports.

The frame spun faster.

I'd like to think the sound I made then was a manly shout of defiance.

The frame spun too far. Snapped out of its support, and had the audacity to thump me on the head as the three of us – myself, and the two parts of that frame – fell towards oblivion.

It was then that I was reminded why I don't entirely discount curses.

This world is a wondrous place. And if you pay attention, you'll find little reminders of that from time to time. Little occurrences that defy expectation or logic.

Like what happened then.

The handrails had broken away. The arch of the frame had broken away. All of that, good, solid wood when this bridge was built.

But the coil of rope that my grappling hook had caught in?

It held.

It held as I fell, unashamedly screaming because I thought I was about to die.

It held as my rope caught me, stealing some of the force of my fall, and keeping my spine from snapping from the sudden tension.

It held as I swung feet-first to the rockface in the direction I was going, and caught myself without even turning an ankle.

And it held as I climbed the sixty feet or so I had to cover to get to the ledge on the far side of that crevasse.

Turned out, of course, that the blades of my grappling hook had cut through the rope and caught on the good, solid stone underneath. There's often a reasonable explanation for weirdness, when you have the time and opportunity to figure it out.

Just the same way that someone dying of a "curse" in an Egyptian tomb probably got caught in a cunning trap, or poisoned by something clever and very, very long-lasting.

But in the moment, that curse probably feels like magic. And in the moment, that ancient rope holding my grappling hook felt like magic.

And that moment of wonder, it's an experience worth remembering.

***

ONCE I WAS SAFELY ON THE OTHER SIDE OF THAT CREVASSE, I NEEDED A break. I parked myself there. Drank some water. Ate one of my chocolate-flavored protein bars, because I needed to feel alive. And a fake chocolate taste is better for that than a fake fruit taste.

Yes, I had some real chocolate with me. I'm not a monster. But I save the real thing for after I'm done. When it's a taste of either celebration or consolation.

No, I didn't know how I was going to get back. I mean, I had ideas about hooking the grapple on the far side and tying off on the near side, but I can't say I liked them much.

But that was a later problem. I still had more exploring to do before I called it a day.

And before I could even do that, I had to do my academic due diligence. More photos, more video – including a verbal explanation of why there were now fewer signs that a bridge had been there – more notes. And then I was making my way farther down that tunnel.

And it was *down* this time. For while I'd been slowly but steadily ascending on my way to the crevasse, I was now slowly but steadily *de*scending on my way away from it.

Which meant that either water had come down from somewhere up that crevasse and cut these two channels that I was calling tunnels, or these tunnels were a human product.

At this point, I was leaning toward the human product answer there. Or at least, that humans had worked on what nature had done first until they were happy with the results.

Or until they abandoned the project...

I mean, whoever took down that bridge – the guy who cut away the rope and slats, not yours truly – did so while *leaving*.

No. No, that bridge had been a labor of love. Too detailed. Weird, in my humble opinion, but detailed all the same. Which suggested that cutting loose the slats had been a temporary measure, not an abandonment of whatever purpose this tunnel had once served.

Well, maybe. I mean, it might have been *intended* as a temporary measure, but I sure couldn't find any signs that the tunnels had seen more use, later.

Perhaps it was abandoned after the death of de la Cruz y Sangre. The locals might've decided that maintaining activity here would only draw more curious Spaniards.

Just something to consider, while I continued on down the tunnel. Which was still quite regular, in terms of spacing and design. Just another reason for me to admit that it was natural.

Someone's hands had shaped this, and done so for a purpose.

Maybe a thousand feet past the crevasse, I found my first signs that the Spaniards had, in fact, gotten this far – a piece of leather belt, and the discarded broken sole of a boot. Both of which had distinctly

European design, as opposed to anything the locals of the era had used.

Of course I photographed, videoed, and logged them extensively before putting them in plastic bags, with my notes.

Felt encouraging, finding those little bits. I'd started to wonder if I'd missed something. Some turn or hidden entrance, maybe concealed along the tunnel walls and left out of the notes.

But no, I was headed the right direction. And I stayed with it.

The tunnel began to curve and level off at the same time. That was different. I think there'd been some gentle curving here and there, along the tunnel, and maybe some parts descended a little quicker than others, but there'd been no *notably different* sections – apart from the chasm – until now.

Now, I could see the tunnel curve to my right, up ahead. And the angle looked to be consistent, as far forward as I could see. No more decline in the path.

Maybe I'd just been hiking for too long through too much sameness, but these little changes were enough to make my stomach flutter. Excitement, or at least hope, began to filter through my tiring muscles. I'd put in a full day's work to get to this point, and normally, by now, I'd be making as much of a camp as I could.

But memories of that Cessna had kept me going. Pushing to make it a little farther today.

Now, I was glad I had.

I slowed a little, as I approached the curve. Took a few pictures of it, just in case.

I started into the curve then, and it was tight. Well, not tight like a *closet*, but for a tunnel cut into a rocky mountain, it was tight. The tunnel itself narrowed to the point that I could touch both walls at the same time. I couldn't see more than ... twenty feet ahead of me before the curve cut my vision.

I was watching the walls, ceiling and floor of the tunnel before I took each step now. I wasn't *expecting* to find any traps, but if there were any, this would be a good place for them. Anyone who got this far would, on instinct, want to speed up, feeling that their goal was close at hand.

Which was exactly the kind of place that people got...

There. In the center of the tunnel floor. Faint outlines of what could be a trapdoor. Or a pit trap.

Only five feet long, which meant I could jump it if I had to. But I didn't want to have to. Grooves went close to the inside wall of the curve, but ... yes, they left about eight inches of lip along the outside. Which designated a safe space for walking, for anyone who knew the trap was there.

I couldn't help but wonder who set it, so I wondered aloud about that as I took video of the outlines and described what I thought it was and why. I also took pictures and notes, before working my way along the safe space to the other side of the danger zone.

I first made sure that I was safe – that there wasn't a second trap following hard on the first – then started recording video again.

"Okay," I said, while training the camera on the presumed danger zone. "I am now going to test if this is, in fact, a pit trap. For anyone watching, I am doing this because I expect to have to come back this way, and don't want to take the chance of not seeing it and falling prey to it. Either because of hurry or distraction."

I paused the recording, and took off my pack. I dug out of it my collapsible titanium pole. It could expand to a length of six feet, and lock into place.

Had to be a thousand uses for that thing.

Anyway, I started recording again, took the pole and gave the danger zone a sharp jab.

First attempt wasn't sharp enough to do anything. So I did it again.

Still nothing.

I drew a deep, steadying breath. I set down the camera and took the pole up in both hands, perpendicular to the tunnel direction. If I fell, the pole would catch between the lip and the tunnel wall, and should support me.

That's right, I was risking this on a "should." But if I discovered, say, a family of hungry jaguars or unleashed the ancient equivalent of mustard gas, I didn't want to risk finding this trap the hard way during a panicked escape attempt.

I stomped hard on the danger zone.

It gave way.

I threw my weight the other direction. Landed hard on the rocky floor of the tunnel, my pole still in hand.

When I got up, heart pounding, panting for breath, I looked over the edge of what was now clearly a hole. I picked up the recorder and gave posterity a good view.

The shaft vanished into darkness. I knew that rocks from the façade covering had fallen, but I didn't hear them hit. Anyone who fell down that shaft would have fallen a very long way.

Interesting that it was set when I encountered it, though. That suggested that either de la Cruz y Sangre had found it and left it intact, or that someone else had reset it.

Disturbing idea. Because that suggested that there might be someone down here, somewhere ahead of me.

And after the noise I just made, they might know I was coming.

---

I TOOK A BREAK, THERE ON THE OTHER SIDE OF THAT APPARENTLY bottomless pit. The idea that there might be people ahead of me somewhere was disturbing. For multiple reasons.

First, because they might kill me on general principle. Either because they expected me to try to exploit them, like de la Cruz y Sangre wanted to do, or simply to keep the outside world from finding out about them at all.

Couldn't blame them for that.

Even if they didn't kill me, though, the presence of living people down here would complicate things a great deal.

I mean, I couldn't just extract the treasure – whatever it was – and bring it to the academics, could I? It's one thing to pluck a jewel from inside a dead mountain. It's another to take it from living hands.

That was a line I wouldn't cross. Best I'd be able to do was take pictures and video of whatever I found.

Assuming I could even do that much. Assuming that the responsible thing wouldn't be to pretend I'd never found any of this in the first place.

And I was assailed by a still worse thought. One I couldn't shake as I rested.

What if living people down here *were* the treasure that de la Cruz y Sangre wrote about?

Sure, he claimed in his notes to have *buried* that treasure down here somewhere, in one of three places. But that could have been a blind, in case of thieves. That would be like him.

And the Spanish invaders *did* take slaves in those days. Not that they were alone in such behavior, but still.

I was beginning to doubt de la Cruz y Sangre's story about burying the treasure anyway. I still hadn't found any significant source of dirt inside this mountain. Some dust, yes. Plenty of that. But nothing that I could call dirt, much less enough of it to bury anything. Plus, I hadn't seen any of the tunnel branches he claimed to have found.

Could've been ahead of me somewhere, I supposed. But...

I shook away the whole line of thought. I'd rested enough. Any more and I'd stiffen up. Might as well get some sleep at that point.

Still staying slow and careful, watching the walls, floor and ceiling before each step, I resumed my course around that curve.

I came to the remnants of a skirmish. Skeletons in decayed tatters of clothes. Old weapons. Looked to have been ... five on two. Locals against Spaniards. Might've been my imagination, but I thought some of the tunnel floor was still discolored from their blood.

I didn't touch any of it.

I stopped and uttered...

All right, look. I've never been a very *religious* man, all right? But I've always considered myself somewhat ... spiritual. And these people, they'd died violent deaths, apparently without anyone reclaiming their remains or performing any kind of funerary rites.

So I gave them a moment of silence, out of respect, then offered a few words to the fallen.

"You who fell here, fighting for what you believe. May you find peace, in whatever follows this life. I will tell your tale."

I took my photos and video then, and wrote all my speculations and conclusions – along with all relevant facts about the discovery and its location – in my notes.

I picked my way across the scene then, disturbing it as little as possible. Partially out of respect for the dead, and partially for the benefit of whatever academics might come investigate this later. Assuming I didn't have to destroy everything I'd learned, to protect some people who wanted no contact with the outside world.

I took a little more video and a few more pictures from the other side, in case the angle mattered. Then I continued on, slowly and carefully, down the tunnel.

I found two more of those pit traps, along the curve. Both of those, though, had already been broken open. I did my due diligence documentation of them, and continued on.

The presence of those two pit traps, along with the remains of that skirmish, had me re-thinking the likelihood of finding anyone living down here. If people were still living somewhere down here, why leave the dead in that tunnel? Why repair one pit trap, but not the other two?

No, the more likely explanation was that, when Zaragoza came back looking for the treasure, he hadn't come alone. But he'd *left* alone, because some of his companions fell into those pit traps, and two more died fighting the locals.

Zaragoza hadn't mentioned bringing any companions into the mountain with him, but that father confessor he'd spoken with, back in Spain, had implied in his own notes that Zaragoza hadn't gone looking for the treasure alone.

Could be, then, that it was Zaragoza himself who cut loose the planks of that bridge, to quell pursuit. Zaragoza's boot, whose heel I'd found. Zaragoza's belt, as well, though how he'd lost a piece of that, I couldn't guess.

Which meant that the first pit trap I'd found hadn't been reset. It simply hadn't been tripped. Zaragoza must've spotted it and either jumped it or skirted the edge, as I had.

These thoughts made me feel better, though. Finding ancient, forgotten treasure, that was my jam. But finding a tribe of forgotten people, that just sounded like a complication I really didn't need.

I don't haunt these forgotten places looking for moral gray areas, you know?

AT THE PLACE WHERE THE CURVE STRAIGHTENED OUT, IT DESCENDED sharply over the course of about a hundred and fifty feet before leveling off again.

And where it leveled off, it led to an opening. An arched opening, that even at a glance from a distance I could tell would be heavily carved and engraved.

The air was warmer now. It had been cool for quite a while. Relative to the heat outside, at least. but now I could feel warmth to it. And a hint of breeze – or some kind of air movement, at least – coming from somewhere past that arch.

The air still smelled mostly dry and dusty, but even that seemed a little different now. Maybe less dry and dusty? Not quite moist, but ... something. Too soon to be sure. And there was some kind of underscent, but not strong enough for me to pick out yet. Not with certainty, anyway, though I did think it might be metallic.

The biggest change, though, was that I could hear something now. For so long, there had been nothing to hear but noises I made. My breath. My heartbeat. The scrape and step of my boots. The slight echo of my own words, when I spoke aloud. The faint whine of electronics when I took pictures or video.

But now, I could hear a faint background roar. A steady sound, that made me think of a distant waterfall. Or maybe a fierce wind, in another tunnel.

When I reached the arch, I stopped to document it as thoroughly as I could. Looking over the carvings...

Yeah, I think it's safe to tell you this much. I don't think it'll clue you in about where I was.

Looking over the carvings, the style didn't strike me as fitting either the Aztecs *or* the Maya. Thematically, maybe. I mean, there were vines and snakes with wings reminiscent of Quetzalcoatl and jaguars and such. But the style didn't quite fit. I'd seen my share of Maya and Aztec art, and this wasn't either. The lines weren't quite right. Something about the thickness and the angles suggested a different hand.

Now, the Aztecs and the Maya weren't the *only* indigenous peoples in Mexico. They're just the main ones you read about, because they dominated a *lot* of area between them. But there were other, smaller groups out there too. Tribes or clans, maybe.

This artwork, it seemed to me to have been done by one of those smaller tribes or clans. So I documented it as thoroughly as I could.

Well, if I found nothing else, my report of this arch might be enough to make some academic's career. Couldn't get too excited about it myself, though, because de la Cruz y Sangre definitely hadn't been writing about it. Which meant it was only an appetizer, with the full meal still to come. If I could find it.

With that thought in mind, I finally allowed myself to consider what I could see past the arch.

The tunnel ended at the arch. There was a lip, or walkway, about ten feet wide, then a drop-off. The drop looked sheer for maybe ... seventy feet, then began curving forward. As though maybe forming a great bowl?

That distant background roar was louder, as I looked down that curving wall. And I could definitely taste a little water on the dry air. Had a be a waterfall down there somewhere. Big one, too, if I was reading the echoes right.

Interesting, considering there weren't any ground level rivers close to this mountain.

Looking up, I couldn't see a ceiling, but I thought I could pick out something, just around the edge of what my light could show. A distant bridge, maybe. Coming out of the wall and disappearing into the darkness.

To my right and left, the walkway looked to describe a slow curve around the edge. As though maybe the outer walls here formed a giant hollow ball, with me inside. All of it still stone. No significant amount of dirt anywhere that I could see yet.

I could definitely feel that warm air moving my direction from the other side of the giant hollow ball.

No. I would not start thinking of this as a giant hollow ball. I wouldn't. So that warm air seemed to be flowing my direction from the other side of this … whatever it was. Architectural center.

Yes. I liked that much better than giant hollow ball. The warm air flowed my direction from the other side of this architectural center.

Well, I had to pick a direction to being exploring. And before I did that, I needed to mark where I'd been. So I pulled out some chalk.

No, not the kind of climbing chalk you might be thinking of. The stuff people use to help give their grip a little more friction. I mean an actual stick of chalk. Like the kind teachers used to use on blackboards, only mine was red.

On the floor in front of the arch, I drew a red X. I planned on following this walkway and finding out more about this giant space, and now I'd have a way to know for certain when I finished a full circuit.

Didn't take long to find another tunnel entrance, also featuring an arch that was just as intricately carved as the first. Though, I noted, with differences. No vines, for example.

The arches at the third and fourth tunnels were different still from the first and second. Which suggested that the differences had significance. Maybe said something about where the tunnels led.

I considered that for a moment. If I was right, then what did it mean that the first tunnel, the one that had led me here, was the only one with any depictions of vines? Could that have been their indicator of which tunnel led outside?

The potential significance of those carvings slowed my circumnavigation. Because I had to go back and start over, fully documenting each arch as I went.

Turned out to be worth my while, though. Because, by going over those arches so thoroughly, I found something I might've missed otherwise.

At the fifth arch, moving to the right from the one that led me here, while taking close-up video of the carvings, I found an anomaly. Along one of the designs, in a section with some right angles, I found what might have been faint dried blood, tracing a calvary cross among the engravings.

Just the kind of thing de la Cruz y Sangre might do, to indicate where he'd hidden whatever treasure he'd found. Hell, "of the Cross and Blood" was his *name*.

I drew a number one on the rocky floor in front of that arch, and kept going. Partially, in case he'd marked more than one. And partially for the sake of completeness.

By the time I finished that circuit, I'd found eight tunnels in all, each of them with intricate carvings on its arch. The fourth from my starting point turned out to be the source of that flow of warm air.

Interestingly, that arch was also the only other arch with vines included in its carvings. If I was right about the meaning of those vines, it might be another possible way out of the mountain.

I didn't find any other anomalies like that blood cross. Though I did find a pair of arching stone bridges that looked to span from one side of the architectural center to the other, crossing each other along the way. Not forming a ninety-degree angle, either, but more like a capital X.

The bridges were all stone. No wood. No rope. And intricately carved, like all the other stonework. In this case, along the railing.

I did have to wonder aloud for a moment why, if they could build such marvelous stone bridges, that first bridge had been built largely from wood and rope. Not something I felt equipped to answer, though. I'd have to leave that for...

For the academics...

I slumped, briefly, in a sigh. I'd have to document those bridges all the way across both of them.

I didn't really want to. I wanted to follow the marked tunnel and find what de la Cruz y Sangre had hidden. But I'd been going out of my way to be good about documenting everything, so I didn't really feel I could just stop doing that.

Besides, it was my dedication to thoroughly documenting this place that had found the blood cross. Maybe following the bridges would find me something too.

Bolstered by that thought, I changed my batteries and mircoSD cards, and got to it.

And it was a good thing I did.

In the center, where the bridges met, was a stone disc maybe twenty feet across. In the center of the disc, a dais featuring an altar, behind which stood a great stone statue with both hands upraised. The statue was manlike in shape, but broad and square-built, rather than an attempt to make it look human. A stylistic choice, I mean. Broad eyes. Open mouth full of stone teeth with tongue hanging out.

The upraised hands were slightly apart...

...as though he'd been holding something.

Something that was most assuredly not there now.

I had to climb the guy to know for sure. He stood about ten feet tall, making his upraised hands almost fifteen feet above the dais with the altar on that disc, but he was an easy climb. And when I got a good look at his hands, I had confirmation.

This stone figure had been holding something. And that something had been pried out and taken away.

That something could only be de la Cruz y Sangre's treasure.

---

Despite the good flutter in my stomach and the excited tension singing through my muscles, I forced myself not to rush off. I kept on with my documenting that center altar – which had too clearly been darkened by blood for my tastes – and made sure to finish documenting the bridges as well. And I took one more circuit of what I was calling the "architectural center," just in case I found any more clues or hints about this treasure.

I did not. I got a lot of pictures and footage that would probably bring academics to ecstasy, but nothing else important to me in the moment.

So, at last, I returned to the tunnel where a small, blood-drawn calvary cross hid among the carvings.

Now, I freely admit. The smart play here would've been to get some sleep. I'd been on the go for a long time. Pushing sixteen, maybe eighteen hours. Maybe more.

But the excitement of the hunt had me now. The idea that I was close to my goal would've made sleep impossible for me anyway. No. I had to push on.

I had to.

That didn't mean, though, that I had to be stupid about it. I forced myself to take another break. Drink a little water. Eat another protein bar – strawberry, or so it claimed to be. And as I did these things, I checked my notes one more time. Hoping that I'd find something in them that would clue me in about how and where de la Cruz y Sangre had hidden his treasure.

Nothing though. Just descriptions of burial places that clearly didn't exist. I had to hope this meant that *all three* of the descriptions were blinds, and that the little blood-drawn cross was his true mnemonic clue about where he'd hidden his find.

Or the first one, at least.

With the expectation that any other hints might be just as subtle, I started down that tunnel. Once more sticking to a slow, steady pace, and checking the tunnel walls, floor and ceiling before every step.

All that extra effort proved to be wasted, this time.

I didn't find any subtle hints or clues.

No, I must've traveled down some eight hundred, maybe a thousand feet of tunnel that way, only to come around a curve and find that the tunnel ahead of me had collapsed.

Collapsed on part of de la Cruz y Sangre's expedition, to boot. A turn of phrase that momentarily made me feel like a bad person, because a pair of ancient leather boots stuck out from inside that pile of rocks. Some poor bastard had been right underneath, when it happened.

Now, you might think that running across a collapsed section of tunnel would make me paranoid about more of it collapsing on me. After all, I'd clearly been concerned about the possibility earlier.

I wasn't worried now, though, for two reasons.

First, clearly, whoever these people were, they *excelled* at stonework. I mean, those crossing bridges were masterworks. Given what I now knew they were capable of, it would have felt obscene to accuse them of making a tunnel that would collapse due to a mistake on their part.

Which brings us to the second reason I wasn't worried.

This collapse was no accident.

It was too ... uniform. Too clean. I could have practically drawn a line across where it started. And I don't just mean on the floor. I could have done it on the walls and ceiling of the tunnel as well.

The poor bastard whose boots I...

Wait.

How was it that *both* his boots were sticking out? I mean, unless the collapse was triggered by a tripwire, and I didn't see how that could be possible. Surely de la Cruz y Sangre's people had been cautious. And it wasn't as though these ancient locals had monofilament wire.

Could have been triggered from somewhere else, maybe. Perhaps this poor soul was chasing a local, and the local threw a lever somewhere on the other side of all these rocks, and buried his pursuer...

...alive.

*Buried.*

This guy wasn't under any dirt. But he was definitely buried.

Which meant that somewhere in this pile of rocks...

I had to check myself from starting to dig right away. I wanted to do this right. So once more I stopped, and took a whole lot of pictures and video. Made some handwritten notes, too. And I didn't say anything on the video about what I hoped to find under the rocks. If I found it, I'd record the find and talk about it then. If not, I didn't want to get anybody's hopes up.

I mean, anybody's but mine. Because my hopes had already broken through the stratosphere on their way out of Earth's gravity well.

Once I'd done my due diligence though, I was ready to start digging.

Side note: doubtless anyone who listened to that recording would be able to tell how excited I was. And since I hadn't mentioned the treasure, they'd probably think I was some kind of sick, demented individual who enjoyed finding a man who'd been crushed to death by falling rocks.

Well, that concern wasn't anything more than a fleeting thought. If any of these academics concluded that I was a sick individual, well, then I figured they were less likely to want to get on my bad side.

Back to what I was doing. Which was documenting.

And while I did that, I assiduously looked for any hints about how or how deep de la Cruz y Sangre had buried his treasure. But there was nothing.

No real surprise, though. A pile of falling rocks can look pretty distinctive, and this one was no exception. Plenty of juts slats versus rounds and so on. Which meant de la Cruz y Sangre might not need any visible clues, so long as he remembered which jut and which rock was the keystone to the hiding place.

I looked over the rock pile, and saw no cross shapes. No indicators. And if it were me, I'm not sure I would have trusted my memory for something so important. I would have found some way to encode...

Encode a key in my notes...

I whipped off my pack and dug out what he'd written down about the three places he claimed to have buried the treasure.

Okay. Here's the thing about interpreting the notes of a paranoid, centuries-dead conquistador. He doesn't write things like, "five paces east, then look for a rock shaped like a jaguar's head, and walk a hundred paces towards it" and yadda yadda yadda.

He writes things like, "I took as many steps as drops of blood shed by Our Lord while they nailed him to the cross."

Yeah.

May not surprise you to learn that there are conflicting accounts of numbers like those. So figuring out the number intended by someone like de la Cruz y Sangre meant first figuring out which accounts he would have had access to, during his lifetime, and which one of *those* he would consider the correct source. Which has to do with knowing when he was writing, and not only who was *pope*, but which cardinals and archbishops would be involved with Spain at the time, not to mention which bishop or bishops a man like de la Cruz y Sangre would have had access to, and would have listened to.

Those last two points, not always the same.

See, figuring these things out, they're the kind of puzzles I was talking about earlier. The kind *I* like to solve. And the reason I can do what I do.

But most people don't have my interest and focus for such things.

So rather than tell you how I reached my conclusions, let me instead tell you this.

De la Cruz y Sangre detailed three different places he might have hidden the treasure he'd found. Each of those detailings was, in fact, a coded system of reminders to himself about where, in this great pile of fallen rocks, he'd buried his found treasure.

Took me a couple of false starts to determine what order the three depictions fell in, in terms of their steps. But finally, I was able to determine precisely where the treasure had been buried.

And those boots sticking out from the rock pile proved to be the key.

That's right. De la Cruz y Sangre was the kind of man to use the body of his own fallen soldier as a clue.

Anyway, as a good person – which that bastard imagined himself to be – is said to follow the right-hand path, the right boot was the missing piece I needed to count up six rocks, over two more, then up to the nearest jutting stone.

From there, I needed only about ten slow, careful minutes of shifting stones about to find it.

And when I did, there was no doubt what I'd found.

This was the moment I loved the most. Excitement carbonated all through my system. Pure joy assailed me as I reached into the hole and drew out my find.

Ornately carved, from what appeared to be a single, giant, emerald of very deep green, a depiction of the sun about seven inches across. And from the bottom of the sun – still part of that dark emerald – jutted a dagger handle big enough to fit into the hands of that stone statue on the altar, with a proportional emerald dagger coming out of that handle.

In all, this thing was almost as long as my *arm. Including* my hand. And its weight was not inconsiderable.

It was a wonder beyond anything I'd ever found before. I tried to imagine those who'd first mined the emerald itself. Then those who'd judged it, chosen it to honor their gods. The craftspeople who'd taken what was naturally magnificent, and rendered from it a work of art for the ages. The pride, they must've felt on finishing.

The joy, their people took in regarding it. And the wonder they must've felt, the religious awe, as it became part of their ceremonies.

Then it was buried. For almost five hundred years, it had gone unseen. Untouched.

Until *I* found it.

That. That was the real reason I did this. That moment of quiet, personal glory. The accomplishment of finding what others hadn't even known was lost. *I* had been the one to puzzle it out. To find and solve the clues. To follow a trail so cold nature had overgrown it at least twice.

And still, I succeeded.

This must've been what Armstrong felt, when he took his first step on the moon.

However, that moment of excitement and wonder never lasted.

And even with the magnificence of this find, it wore off all too quickly.

Then, alas, came the mundane necessity of documenting the Emerald Sun Dagger, as I was calling it in my head, as well as how I found it and how I broke the cypher of de la Cruz y Sangre's notes. I went into the full description of the artifact itself as well, even though they could see it.

I closed the narrative portion of my documentation with thoughts about why de la Cruz y Sangre had buried it the way he did. Or at least, why he chose to bury it rather than bring it back out with him, when he got called out to fight off the locals.

Wasn't as though he could have hidden this thing. And if any of the locals had seen it in his hands – given its likely religious significance – they would have fought all the harder.

No, from his viewpoint, it was probably smarter to leave it here and come back for it later.

Later never came for de la Cruz y Sangre. He died before ever bringing this treasure out into the light.

Sobering thought. And a mistake I had no intention of repeating.

Which meant it was time for me to get some sleep.

Before I did that, though, I buried the Emerald Sun Dagger right where it had been before.

Just in case.

———

I ALWAYS SLEEP A LITTLE MORE SOUNDLY AFTER A GREAT FIND. EVEN when I'm sleeping in a rocky tunnel deep inside a mountain, tasting air that was cool, dusty and mostly dry. Mostly, only because it was slightly moistened by that waterfall somewhere down deep in the architectural center.

Pity the waterwall wasn't closer. I could've done with a shower and some fresh water. I still had water in my canteens, but there's nothing like drinking it fresh, straight from a waterfall.

Ah well. At least the distant, faint roar from that waterfall had been pleasant enough to sleep to. Kind of like a white noise generator. Helped me get maybe … four hours of actual sleep. Couldn't ask for more than that. Not eager as I was to see my find get safely where it needed to go.

This felt like the find of my career. And I knew it.

A thought that helped jolt me fully awake again. Made me bolt down another faux-cherry protein bar – this time supplemented with an apple, as a reward for my find – and some of that canteen water. Then, sticking to routine so I avoided cramps and strains, which could prove fatal down here, I stretched and limbered up my muscles.

Next, I dug out the Emerald Sun Dagger.

I will admit it. I sighed in relief that it was still there.

Funny thing, really. No matter how many times I did something like this, it still happened. I made my find just before going to sleep, and woke up the following morning worried that it had all been just a dream.

So I sighed in relief, and a part of me unclenched as I pulled the Emerald Sun Dagger back out of its hiding place.

Couldn't wait to see this wonder in real, natural sunlight, as opposed to the light of my LED headlamp. I mean, sure, I set my lamp to *emulate* natural sunlight, but the truth was that there was no replacement for the real thing.

Not to mention that the real thing was much stronger.

Carrying the Emerald Sun Dagger wouldn't be that big a deal, in terms of weight, but it would be hard to conceal. And I knew that, once I got out of the mountain once more, concealment would become very important.

Not just because of my *competitors*, either. Though memories of that Cessna still troubled me.

No, I'd be leaving this mountain carrying the biggest honking emerald I'd ever *heard* of. And it was that lovely dark color that made it even more valuable than its size and detailed carvings would make it on their own.

In other words, anyone with any kind of … casual relationship with the law would be only too happy to relieve me of my prize. And I could *not* let that happen.

I'd had my moment of joy in finding the Emerald Sun Dagger. Now came the responsibilities that accompanied the find. Possibly the most significant find of my career.

I *had* to get this thing to the right hands. ASAP. I owed it to history. To those who'd made this wonder in the first place. To all those who shared in its heritage, and the heritage of those people who'd once come deep into this mountain to perform their rites.

When I came back out of this tunnel and once more into the architectural center of all these tunnels, I made sure to wipe away the number one I'd drawn. The academics would find the tunnel just fine from the material I'd be giving them. No reason to leave an unnecessary mark for anyone *else* who came through.

I also erased the X I'd drawn on the rocky floor at the mouth of the tunnel that had led me here in the first place.

As I did that, I felt that soft, warm breeze blowing from across the way. That breeze, what there was of it, tempted me. Tempted me to see where it led. Because I suspected it also led out of the mountain. And that would be good information to have. Not to mention that there might be more to find along the way.

Couldn't do it, though, tempted as I was. Not while carrying the Emerald Sun Dagger. If I came out somewhere else on the mountain, I might not have cover nearby. I'd risk being too exposed, if that Cessna was still looking for me. Not to mention that I'd need too long to get to my tent.

No, I needed to get out of the mountain and out of the wilderness at best speed. So I would have to leave the mysteries of that tunnel and its warm breeze for another to discover.

I started back. Picking my way carefully past the skirmish scene, and the open pit traps. Forcing myself to keep a steady, measured pace during the long stretches of tunnel where I knew I'd find nothing but steps between myself and where I needed to go.

It was tempting, for stretches like those, to pick up the pace. I knew it was safe. I knew I wouldn't ruin anything. So I felt the urge to hustle past and be on my way.

But I had too far to go. I couldn't risk burning out too soon. That might leave me tired and slow, when strength and speed inevitably became important.

So I fought that urge and hummed one of my dad's old Navy cadences to keep my steps even and at a reasonable pace.

It was a good plan. And it sustained me all the way to that busted bridge.

A busted bridge I had to...

Cold fear whipped through my system. I doused my light and ducked down behind the stonework at the base of what had once been that wood-and-rope bridge, spanning this chasm.

I tucked down there and waited.

Because I'd seen light on the other side. The bright, vivid white LED light used by people who didn't care how natural their light source looked.

Nerves made me jumpy enough to shake, so I calmed through slow, steady breaths. One at a time. In through the nose, out through the mouth. Over and over.

A little steadier now, I hid there. Waiting. Peeking around one edge.

The light grew closer.

Closer.

I could hear the trod of multiple pairs of feet now. The echoes of two or three voices, though no sense of what they were saying, or even what language they were speaking.

The light split into six sources as they emerged from the tunnel at the other side of the chasm. I could hear them clearly now, through the echoes. Speaking English. Complaining. About the drop. About the state of the bridge. In fact, it took them a moment to say anything interesting, but when they did, they mentioned me by name.

"Obviously Taggart didn't come this way."

"Had to've," another said, that that was a voice I recognized. Quintus Menon. Just about my dad's age, a shock of white hair against a tan darker than mine, and so full of bile his whole body sagged with it.

Couldn't believe Menon came this far himself. Couldn't believe he'd managed to drag his fat ass up the mountainside. What'd they do, air lift him?

But Menon was still talking.

"No way Taggart buries his tent unless he has a find very close by. That four-foot cross just *reeks* of conquistador work, and that the opening up the mountainside wasn't obvious from the ground just cements it."

Son of a bitch shook his head and looked around as though he expected to see me.

Okay, I'll admit, I pulled a little more into the shadows on my side then, and settled for listening instead of looking.

"No," he finished. "Taggart came this way."

"And what do you think he did here, *fly*?" So much disdain in that voice that I had to sneak a peek at the speaker. This silly bastard looked like six feet of muscle. I could hear the slight remnants of an Australian accent he'd clearly tried to lose.

Silly Bastard continued as I drew back. "You said he only worked alone, and that he was cautious. A cautious man who works alone does *not* try to cross this chasm."

"Maybe he did," said another. "Maybe he tried, failed, and fell."

"Don't be stupid," Silly Bastard said. "We'd find some sign. Maybe his grappling hook."

"Not if it didn't catch right. See that rope around the rocks on the other side?"

I froze, entirely too close to some of that rope for comfort.

"Yeah," Silly Bastard said.

"Well, maybe his grapple caught on the rope, not the rock. Maybe it slipped out when he tried to cross, and—"

"It's easily sixty feet across," Silly Bastard said.

"So?"

"So if he tried that without tying off at this end, he'd have to swing sixty feet and try to catch himself on rock, on the other side. Great way to sprain an ankle or blow out a knee. Cautious man wouldn't do it. Cautious man doesn't try to cross here *at all*. But if he *has* to, he anchors himself very well on this end, and maybe tries climbing across after being *very* sure how well his grappling hook caught on the other side."

That ... actually was my first thought about how to get back.

Maybe Silly Bastard wasn't so silly after all. Couldn't just call him Bastard in my head, though. I mean, I didn't even know the guy.

*Menon* I could've called Bastard. He'd more than earned it. But I *knew* his name.

"Obviously Taggart didn't do that," Menon said. "My local agents assure me he didn't know he was followed, ergo he wasn't expecting us—"

"He buried his tent," Silly Bastard said.

"Yes," Menon said, irritated at the interruption, "but I suspect he does that out of habit, whether he thinks he needs to or not."

A fair assessment, I had to admit.

"If he had crossed as you suspect, anchoring on the far side with his grappling hook and on this side by tying off, he would have left his escape route in place, rather than waste resources by cutting free his hook."

"You sound like you have another option," Silly Bastard said.

"Of course I do. I suspect some portion of this bridge was yet intact when he reached this point. I suspect he attempted to cross it, after first anchoring himself to the far side with his grappling hook. He likely crossed some portion of the bridge before it gave out, but give out it did, descending down below and out of sight."

All right, look. I never said Menon wasn't a *smart* bastard.

"Leaving him falling," Silly Bastard said thoughtfully. "But his grappling hook held, he had a good dynamic rope to steal some of his momentum, and he didn't have to fall as far toward the chasm wall. Maybe had shortened the distance enough to save his knees and ankles."

"Precisely," Menon said, and I didn't have to see him to know he'd given a nod to emphasize his point. It was just the sort of thing he did.

"One problem," Silly Bastard said.

"Oh?"

"That's a lot of risk for a cautious man."

"It is indeed," Menon said, voice smiling with avarice. "Too *much* risk. Unless the *reward* was even greater. No, gentlemen. Taggart crossed here, and so shall we. And unlike our erstwhile quarry, we shall do so with safety and stability."

Did I mention I really hate this guy? Because I do. I *really* do.

---

Took Menon's people a little time to get set up, before they were ready to do their thing. I, of course, couldn't watch them. They were doing their level best to bathe my side of the chasm with as much obnoxiously white light as they could – to ease their trip across – while I was doing *my* level best to keep them from seeing *me* in the process.

Soon enough though, I heard hammering. Pitons into stone was my guess. I was close. I wasn't quite right, though, and I knew it as soon as I heard that sound.

I think – and I've never used them myself, so I'm not certain, but I *think* – the kind of gun they fired uses a type of compressed gas to power its projectile. Definitely not gunpowder. Not nearly loud enough. Or sharp enough. The sound that kind of gun makes when it fires – which was what I heard then – is more of *whump*.

Certainly generated plenty of oomph. Because the metal projectile – looked kind of like a short spear, with attachments – slammed hard into the chasm wall beside the tunnel entrance, driving deep. Maybe ... five-and-a-half feet above the lip, and maybe ten feet from my hiding place, on the other side of the stone base of what had once been a bridge.

Metal spear looked to be barbed, suggesting that it now provided a *solid* anchor. Which it would need, to support the rope and two pulleys that were attached to the haft.

Yep. These guys were going to anchor the other end of that rope –

probably with a second set of pulleys – and basically zipline their way across.

It was a good approach. I *almost* wished I'd thought of it.

Except, of course, that it required *way* too much equipment for me to carry on my lonesome.

Price of working alone, and I'd keep on paying it, thank you.

Problem was, that meant that all six of those guys would very soon be joining me on *this* side. Which was pretty much the worst possible outcome for me.

Well, Menon wouldn't *kill* me. After all, if he did, he'd have to do his *own* research rather than trying to steal *my* finds. But he'd still make off with the Emerald Sun Dagger, and that I couldn't allow.

But I couldn't take off down the tunnel, either. I'd waited too long. They'd see me. And they'd likely catch me.

Which meant that it was time for the cautious man to once more do something ... inadvisable.

My pack probably weighed about ... forty pounds or so at that point. Not counting the Emerald Sun Dagger, I mean. That thing added ... whuf, I'm not sure. Psychology plays tricks on you, trying to gauge some things. I knew it was heavy, and I *want* say it weighed maybe another thirty pounds or so, but I can't be sure of that.

Assuming that was right, then I was carrying about seventy pounds on my back. A lot of weight to add to my own, for what I had in mind. Had to hope my muscles were up to the task.

Quietly as I could, when it sounded as though the first interloper was getting ready to come over, I opened two hooks of my grapple. I wished I had static rope tied to it for this, but that couldn't be helped. My dynamic rope was still attached after my last use.

I picked the best, most stable spot I could, setting my hooks among the rocky surface at the foot of the stonework that had once formed one end of that bridge.

I snuck a glance around the stonework. Saw one of Menon's people starting across, while the others were strapping on clip harnesses for their turn.

Their attention was on each other, and their way across. This was the best shot I'd get.

I slipped the loose end of my rope through the loops I wore for that purpose, and tied off. With that done, quietly as I could, I crawled toward the far edge, away from the zipline, playing out my rope as I went.

Then, over the edge I went. Not much more than a few feet, because distance wouldn't help. They'd see me or they wouldn't. One thing I could do though, was spread my feet to control my position and keep myself in place.

Movement draws the human eye faster than anything else. Faster than colors. Faster than shapes. Movement.

And I gave their eyes as little movement to work with as I could, while silently offering a request to those ancients whose work I was trying to honor. If there was an afterlife, maybe they'd take pity on me. Or at least maybe they'd recognize Menon and his people as far more like de la Cruz y Sangre than I was.

Honestly, though, I think I did it because silently talking to ghosts was the only productive thing I could think of to do. I didn't even want to watch them cross. Couldn't risk exposing the chance of eye contact.

My heart pounded. Adrenaline blitzed my system, which was both good and bad. Good, in that it helped my muscles support me through this. Bad, in that I had to fight against the shakes to keep myself still.

One by one I listened to them come over and detach themselves.

One by one, they immediately started investigating the tunnel on the other side.

The skirmish!

Oh, Menon would *loot* that skirmish for antiques.

Oh, well, better that he find those than the Emerald Sun Dagger. At least I documented it first.

Hey! My photos and video might even help Mexican authorities go after Menon, when he tried to *move* those antiques...

Speak of the devil, Menon was now crossing. Second-to-last. I knew he'd arrived because I heard him start talking while he was still detaching.

"Split up. I want a pair of scouts pushing two hundred feet down that tunnel. And be careful. If Taggart even *suspected* that we're on his tail, he might leave one or two of the ancient traps unsprung, waiting for us.

"You're just assuming he'd find them?" That was Silly Bastard, who'd taken charge of the others pending Menon's arrival.

They continued talking as they started down the tunnel, while the last member of their party was still unstrapping.

"You don't know Taggart," Menon said. "He's the sort to have researched the kind of traps these people would use. And even if he doesn't know we're following, he'd likely leave at least one intact for those scholars he loves so much."

They were out of earshot then. And I listened while the tread of the last of their people followed.

I didn't let out an easy breath, though, for another two hundred heartbeats. Just to be safe.

Then struggling against all that extra weight, I climbed back to the ledge and peeked. Half-expecting to see Menon and his people looking at me. Smiling.

They weren't there, though. They were gone.

And they'd left me a convenient means of crossing the chasm, when they left.

Good of them. My arms needed a break.

Me, I wasn't feeling so charitable. So I cut their rope before I sped off down the tunnel toward the outside world.

---

By the way, I don't think it was the ghosts of ancient people blinding Menon's group to my presence that kept them from noticing me. And I don't think it was that I'd picked some perfect hiding spot.

No, I've had a lot of time to think about this, since that day, and I think I know why they didn't see me.

They didn't expect to.

See, they'd been chasing me, yes. But they'd already looked for me on that lip of stone, while looking across the chasm, and not found me. So they assumed I wasn't there to find. That I was somewhere ahead of them, down the tunnel.

A reasonable conclusion, to be honest. I was certainly doing my best to keep them from finding out I was on my way back.

And once they'd decided I wasn't there to find, they'd shifted their focus entirely to crossing the chasm and heading down the tunnel.

If even *one* of them had stopped and given my side a once-over before moving on, they'd've found me.

But they didn't expect to find me. They didn't expect to find *anything* on that lip. And the tunnel ahead of them, *that* was unexplored territory. Where they might find treasures I'd missed, or maybe even their quarry.

So they pushed on, and missed spotting my little, half-open grappling hook, and the trail of soft gray rope that would have led them right to me.

That's what I think happened, anyway. Though to be honest, it's more fun to think that the ghosts of ancients blinded the evil men to my presence.

Anyway, once I recrossed the chasm, I just had to make my way through the tunnel and back to the entrance.

I stopped there at the entrance, with the overhang above me and the huge, jutting rock between me and any more of Menon's people who might be waiting down below.

Mind you, logically, I didn't think Menon could have anybody else with him. Considering he came here in that Cessna, I was surprised Menon had as many as *five* people with him. I mean, a Cessna seats two in most configurations, and adding more weight was *not* going to help any with takeoffs and landings.

But logic was for research. In the field, I had to trust my gut.

And my gut told me to hang back and sneak a peek.

Midday sun overhead, which was just not fair. I'd be coming out into prostration-level heat, and I was already on the tired side, from all the miles, effort, and adrenaline that'd gotten me this far.

Menon had a whole camp set up. Four tents. Fire pit. A beige, military-style truck. The kind that looks as though it's made by Jeep, whether it was or not.

So I guess not everyone flew in.

And not everyone went into the mountain, either. One guy stayed behind to stand guard. Or sit guard, really. He looked kind of like an ex-military type, but gone to seed.

Still, he had a pistol on his hip, and a walkie-talkie on his belt. Walkie-talkie probably wasn't a problem. Menon and his other people were too far into the mountain by now to be in range.

But that pistol was another matter.

I huddled there, near the edge, and watched for a while. Had to make sure no one else came out of those tents. Or maybe came back in from patrol.

No one did, though.

I could get down the mountainside pretty quickly, when the time came. No, not by falling. Menon's people had set up a climbing ladder, but I wouldn't use that either. Much faster to use my grappling hook and rope. Rappel my way down. It would mean abandoning that grapple and rope, but I didn't see much choice. I'd have to abandon my tent too, and the rest of my food and water.

Again, didn't see much of a choice. But I had an idea about how to keep my course of action from becoming lethal.

If it was going to work, though, I had to pick the right time to make my move. Last thing I wanted to do was let Mr. Pistol take me captive.

I knew what to wait for, though, and it was just a matter of time before my opportunity came.

See, Menon fancied himself a very civilized man. Which meant he set a civilized camp. Which meant that Mr. Pistol would have to *leave* that camp to take a leak.

And a little while later, that was what he did.

I made my move. Rappelled down the mountainside just as fast as

I could, then hustled to the far side of the big rock from where I'd left my tent.

I was tempted to rest there. Gather myself. But I couldn't. Soon as Mr. Pistol spotted that rope – which he might, if he looked up to see if his people were coming back – he'd be after me.

I did have to take long enough to orient myself, though. With the midday sun directly overhead, I didn't have it as a directional clue, and I needed a moment to remember that I'd entered Gold Mountain on its *north* face. Which meant that, from my meager hiding place with my back to that big rock, I was facing *east*.

Now, this next part is part of the reason I have such a good rep for research.

See, I knew *I* wouldn't be flying in. I only did that when absolutely necessary. Flight logs were too easy to spy on, for *competitors* with enough money. Of which I had more than my share.

But I knew those same *competitors* would fly in, if they came after me.

So before coming here, I'd noted the three best places to land a Cessna anywhere *close* to the area where I expected to find Gold Mountain.

And of those, I knew Menon would choose not the easiest, but the closest. After all, this was a man who would make his own date drop him off at a restaurant's door, rather than walk two hundred steps from the parking lot under his own power.

And that landing strip, from here was...

North by northeast.

I pulled out my knife. Not the little utility one, but the big Ka-bar that had come in handy more times than I cared to count. I held it so the blade tucked up along my forearm.

Once ready, I started moving. Walking as though I belonged there and had left something in the truck.

I was almost to the truck when he noticed me.

"Collins?"

I waved noncommittally without looking back.

"What'd Big Man forget?"

Again without looking back, I made sounds that I hoped would come across as unclear English. Didn't want to tip anything with true intonation or pronunciation.

Right around the time I reached the truck, Mr. Pistol spoke again.

"Collins?" This time, he sounded suspicious. "Answer me."

That last carried a weight to it. A command. And a confidence that told me he'd drawn that pistol.

I glanced into the truck.

Alas, the keys weren't in it.

But then, I didn't really expect them to be. I never got that lucky.

Pretending to reach into the open back of the truck, I instead slammed my knife hilt-deep into a tire.

"Hey!" Mr. Pistol yelled. But he must not've had an angle, because he didn't start firing.

I took that as my cue. Yanked the knife back out, but couldn't take time to savor the tire's death-hiss.

I started running. Broken-field running. Ducking as low as I could while still putting as much distance between us as I could for when...

I heard the echoing report of a 9mm, followed quickly by a *sprang* and chips of rock flying from the ground much closer than I liked.

*Much closer than I liked.* Look who's trying to sound brave.

Truth was, that shot probably hit ... four yards to my right. But it felt in the moment as though he'd missed my head by six inches. And my tired legs poured on greater speed under that blazing sun, while my balls tried to climb back up into my body for safety. And honestly, puckered as my sphincter was in that moment, I'm surprised I could run at all.

But that gunshot, that did great things for speeding my heartbeat and distributing adrenaline through my body. Stark, mortal terror works wonders that way. Don't know how fast I was really going, but I sure felt as though I could've outrun Usain Bolt.

I already had a good forty, maybe forty-five yards between us when he took that first shot. Which meant that Mr. Pistol had the choice between shooting on the run – trying to maintain a steady distance – or setting himself for accuracy over a longer distance and risking my getting away.

Accuracy with a 9mm is a tricky thing, at distances much longer than fifty yards. And Mr. Pistol must've known that. He took one more shot – which didn't come as close as the first – then started after me.

But this guy, he'd gone to seed more than a little. And I kept myself fighting trim, doing crazy stuff like this. So I figured my chances of losing this guy were pretty good.

Unfortunately, either I'd underestimated Mr. Pistol's conditioning, or Menon's discipline. Because that bastard stayed with me as I ran across the rocky ground through the foothills between mountains and around a curve to might right and into the channel – small valley, if you like – where I expected to find Menon's Cessna.

And there it was. A dusky orange-red thing of beauty. Under the circumstances, anyway.

Pushing for one last sprint, I ran straight for that plane.

———

OKAY. IF YOU'RE GOING TO BELIEVE THIS NEXT PART, I'M GOING TO HAVE to tell you something I don't like admitting to. Because if it gets back to my *competitors*, it won't work anymore. So I have to hope you're going to keep this to yourself.

You will, I hope?

Well, you'd probably say yes either way, so I might as well push on.

Back, oh, let's just say a few years ago, I did some research into Cessnas. Not just the planes themselves, but their parts. And who *manufactured* those parts. With particular emphasis on the locks used for their cabin doors and ignitions.

And with that information, I called in a favor or two and had some skeleton keys made. Which means that I can get into and start pretty much any Cessna I come across.

I don't abuse this, actually. Never stole a plane. Never even took one joyflying. Though arguably, I was about to do one or the other. Depending on who's telling the story.

No, the only times I'd used those keys in the past had been to enter the Cessnas of a couple of *competitors* and retrieve certain things they'd stolen from me.

Well, all right. I did once pee on Hanover's parachute. But he *more* than had it coming, believe you me.

Anyway, as I reached the Cessna, I heard Mr. Pistol yell something short and sharp. Probably "Stop!" or "Halt!" or something along those lines. The kind of thing people yell even when they *know* that the person they're yelling at will *not* do what they want.

He took another shot at me, and came closer than I liked. Which meant that the rocky chips kicked up were within ten feet of me.

I quickly unlocked the plane, clambered inside, and locked it behind me. Fast as I could, I strapped my pack into the copilot's seat and started up the preflight sequence while claiming the pilot's seat.

Mr. Pistol was waving his arms at me now, trying to get my attention, while yelling something intended to be attention grabbing. Probably "Hey!" again, or something equally effective.

The question I had was, was this guy stupid enough to shoot Menon's plane?

He wasn't. And I was just getting the plane moving, taxiing to turn around for takeoff, when he pulled out his walkie-talkie.

I immediately heard his voice, over the radio. Guess they'd left it tuned to their chosen channel.

"Do you have any idea how big a crime *plane theft* is down here?"

A wise man probably would've ignored him. But though I liked to think I was cautious, I'd never claimed to be the *wisest* man around.

"Probably not as big as *murder*," I answered. "And this isn't theft. This is doing what I have to, to save my own life. Escaping from a maniac with a gun, who is actively trying to kill me."

"All right. All right." I heard a clattering sound. "I've dropped the gun. I'll kick it away as soon as you kill the engines."

"Pull the other one. It's got bells on."

I throttled up, and started down the runway.

"Wait! Taggart! That *is* you, right? The guy Menon's looking for?"

"You mean you weren't even *sure* when you tried to murder me?"

"Taggart, don't leave me here. Do you know what Menon will *do* to me if I let you escape?"

I hesitated at that. I didn't know. But Menon could be ruthless. I knew that much...

No. This was a trick. Had to be.

"Nice try. I stop the plane, you meet me at the door, gun in hand and smile on your face."

"It's not a trick! I swear!"

"Then change the tire and drive away, you're so worried."

He didn't answer that, which told me all I needed to know.

I throttled up hard and took to the air just as he started shooting again.

He did put a hole in his boss' Cessna, but I got away.

---

Turned out that Mr. Pistol's final shot may have saved me significant jail time.

See, air traffic controllers don't like it when small planes without registered flight paths disrupt their carefully balanced schedule for an unscheduled landing. Especially not at big airports, like the one in Mexico City.

In situations like those, air traffic controllers send not just any cops to come talk to you. They send the kind of cops whose authority is just this side of *divine*. The kind of cops who can and will lock you away for a very long time, if they have a reason to. The kind of cops who know just what to say to the American embassy, so that the U.S. won't raise even a *breath* of complaint about it, either.

About a dozen of these cops were waiting when I landed, led by a man named Captain Chapulin. Captain Chapulin looked half-Aztec himself, along with enough wrinkles and gray hair to let me know there was no lie in those eyes that said he'd seen everything, and had yet to be impressed by any of it.

But cops like those, they get their jobs by being damned good at what they do.

So even before I'd set down, they'd seen the bullet hole Mr. Pistol had put in the fuselage.

And that bullet hole, it lent credence to the true story I'd already told those air traffic controllers. Yes, that bullet hole, I'm pretty sure it helped convince Captain Chapulin to actually *listen* when I started talking.

Might've helped that I was speaking Spanish. Helped avoid the "typical American" stereotypes.

Mind you, the moment those cops saw the Emerald Sun Dagger – which they did when they went through my stuff while I was talking – I had guns pointed at me again.

Big a deal as that object was, it moved the conversation inside. Into air conditioned offices – all right, interrogation rooms – and away from the chances of random strangers seeing that giant honking emerald artifact.

In fact, things might've looked really bad for me at that point. Because I was now in the kind of place where arresting me was a matter of a couple of forms, rather than effort.

So I made sure they found *all* my documentation. All my photos and video and notes. They found those bits of boot and belt, as well as those rope fibers – in their plastic bags – along with the cards describing them and where I'd found them.

All of that led to the question I'd been hoping to get asked.

Captain Chapulin looked me in the eye, across a steel table painted lime green, and said, "If you're not just another thief here to steal artifacts, then you must have someone who can vouch for you. Who?"

Ah, the question of who could vouch for me. Which was one of the benefits of turning over every find to the academics, rather than just selling to the highest bidder.

Those academics, they *would* vouch for me. Especially the ones I'd given a find to in the past. Like, say, Professor Julio Rodriguez, chair of the History department at the prestigious National Autonomous University of Mexico. Right here in Mexico City.

That's right. My choice to land in Mexico City had a purpose.

Professor Rodriguez was no little name to throw around, either. Very influential man. Enough so that Captain Chapulin had a phone brought in and called him right from the interrogation table.

When Professor Rodriguez heard who Captain Chapulin was holding for questioning, he got so excited I could hear his response, even though the phone wasn't on speaker.

*"Clark Taggart is here in Mexico?"* he said, in Spanish. *"What new wonder has he dug up for us this time?"*

I couldn't help myself. I answered loudly. *"It's me, Julio. And I've been calling it the Emerald Sun Dagger. You have to see this thing. And I got you lots of great pictures and video, too. A whole mountain full of passages you'll love, including carvings, marvelous stone bridges, and at least one statue."*

I turned to Captain Chapulin. "Remember what I told you about Quintus Menon? He and his people are in that mountain right now. And they *will* steal what they find, if they get a chance."

Professor Rodriguez kept talking loudly. *"Quintus Menon? Did he say Quintus Menon? Captain, Quintus Menon is a known artifact thief and international menace. You have to stop him!"*

*"I'll make some calls,"* Captain Chapulin said. *"And thank you, professor. You've been most helpful. Yes, I'll make sure Mr. Taggart has guards when he brings you the artifact. I'll see to it personally."*

The captain smiled at me now, and that smile was the best thing I'd seen all day.

He even switched to English, which felt like a compliment.

"Mr. Taggart, you have had a very long, hard day. But if you don't mind it getting a little longer, after we bring that artifact to Professor Rodriguez, I would very much like to buy you dinner. And if you're willing, while we eat, perhaps you will tell me the story of how you came to find that wonder in the first place."

"Captain," I said with a smile, "it would be my pleasure."

# SIGN UP FOR STEFON'S NEWSLETTER

Stefon loves to keep in touch with his readers, and loves to keep you reading. The best way for him to do both is for you to sign up for his newsletter.

Sign up at http://www.stefonmears.com/join

If you sign up for Stefon's newsletter, you get...

- Monthly updates about his publishing and travel schedules
- His latest news, in brief, and answers to reader questions
- A free short story for signing up
- List-only offers and occasional specials
- Plus a free short story every month!

# ABOUT THE AUTHOR

Stefon Mears would love to discover some hidden site and treasure. Stefon has more than thirty novels to his credit, and he never stops writing. He earned his M.F.A. in Creative Writing from N.I.L.A., and his B.A. in Religious Studies (double emphasis in Ritual and Mythology) from U.C. Berkeley. He's a lifelong gamer and fantasy fan. Stefon lives in Portland, Oregon, with his wife and three cats.

*Look for Stefon online:*
www.stefonmears.com
himself@stefonmears.com

www.ingramcontent.com/pod-product-compliance
Lightning Source LLC
Chambersburg PA
CBHW030907200726
48289CB00003B/935